SKYWALKER STRIKES: VOLUME 3

It is a period of renewed hope for the Rebellion. The evil Galactic Empire's greatest weapon, the Death Star, has been destroyed, and now the Rebel Alliance looks to press its advantage by unleashing a daring offensive throughout the far reaches of space.

Princess Leia Organa has led a covert team of rebels in an attack on Cymoon 1, the largest weapons factory in the galaxy. But after rigging the factory's main power core to explode and rescuing dozens of innocent slave workers, their escape plan was thwarted by the unexpected arrival of Darth Vader.

Now the rebels must fight their way to freedom, using the Empire's own vehicles as their means of escape. And Luke Skywalker must remain one step ahead of the unstoppable Lord Vader, who is beginning to take an interest in the young rebel pilot....

JASON AARON
Writer

JOHN CASSADAY
Artist

LAURA MARTIN
Colorist

CHRIS ELIOPOULOS
Letterer

CASSADAY & MARTIN
Cover Artists

CHARLES BEACHAM
Assistant Editor

JORDAN D. WHITE
Editor

**C.B. CEBULSKI &
MIKE MARTS**
Executive Editors

**AXEL
ALONSO**
Editor In Chief

**JOE
QUESADA**
Chief Creative Officer

**DAN
BUCKLEY**
Publisher

For Lucasfilm:
Creative Director MICHAEL SIGLAIN
Senior Editor JENNIFER HEDDLE
Lucasfilm Story Group RAYNE ROBERTS, PABLO HIDALGO,
LELAND CHEE

ABDO
Spotlight

ABDOPUBLISHING.COM

Reinforced library bound edition published in 2017 by Spotlight,
a division of ABDO, PO Box 398166, Minneapolis, Minnesota 55439.
Spotlight produces high-quality reinforced library bound editions for
schools and libraries. Published by agreement with Marvel Characters, Inc.

Printed in the United States of America, North Mankato, Minnesota.
042016
092016

THIS BOOK CONTAINS
RECYCLED MATERIALS

marvelkids.com

PUBLISHER'S CATALOGING IN PUBLICATION DATA

Names: Aaron, Jason, author. | Cassaday, John ; Martin, Laura, illustrators.
Title: Star Wars : Skywalker strikes / by Jason Aaron ; illustrated by Laura Martin
and John Cassaday.
Description: Minneapolis, MN : Spotlight, [2017] | Series: Star Wars : Skywalker
strikes
Summary: Luke Skywalker and the ragtag rebels opposing the Galactic Empire are
fresh off their biggest victory so far-the destruction of the massive Death Star!
But the Empire's not toppled yet! Join Luke, Princess Leia, Han Solo,
Chewbacca, C-3PO, R2-D2, and the rest of the Rebel Alliance as they fight for
freedom against Darth Vader and his evil master, the Emperor!
Identifiers: LCCN 2016932364 | ISBN 9781614795278 (v.1 : lib. bdg.) | ISBN
9781614795285 (v.2 : lib. bdg.) | ISBN 9781614795292 (v.3 : lib. bdg.) | ISBN
9781614795308 (v.4 : lib. bdg.) | ISBN 9781614795315 (v.5 : lib. bdg.) | ISBN
9781614795322 (v.6 : lib. bdg.)
Subjects: LCSH: Skywalker, Luke (Fictitious character)--Juvenile fiction. | Star Wars
fiction--Comic books, strips, etc.--Juvenile fiction. | Graphic novels--Juvenile
fiction.
Classification: DDC 741.5--dc23
LC record available at http://lccn.loc.gov/2016932364

Spotlight

A Division of ABDO
abdopublishing.com

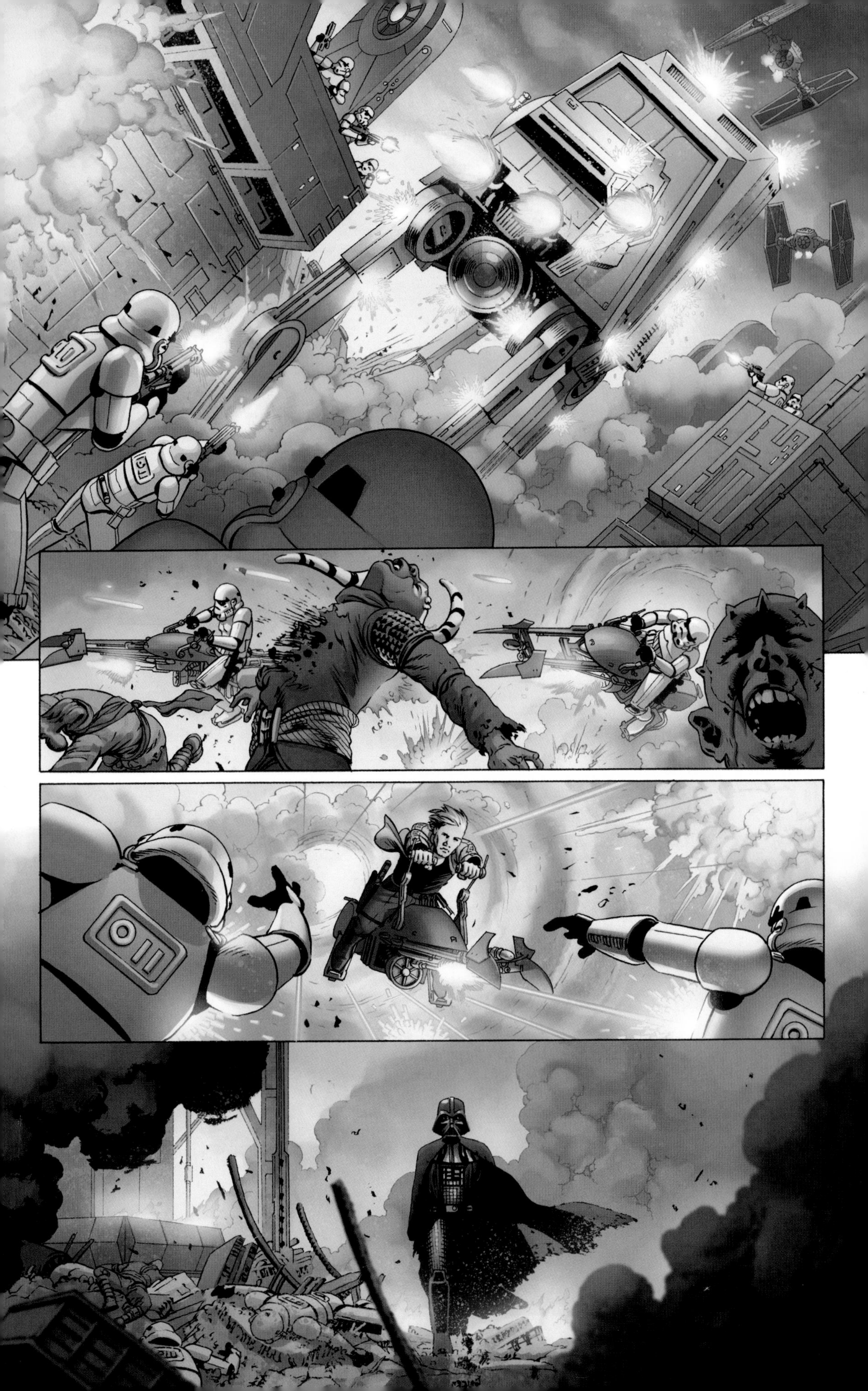

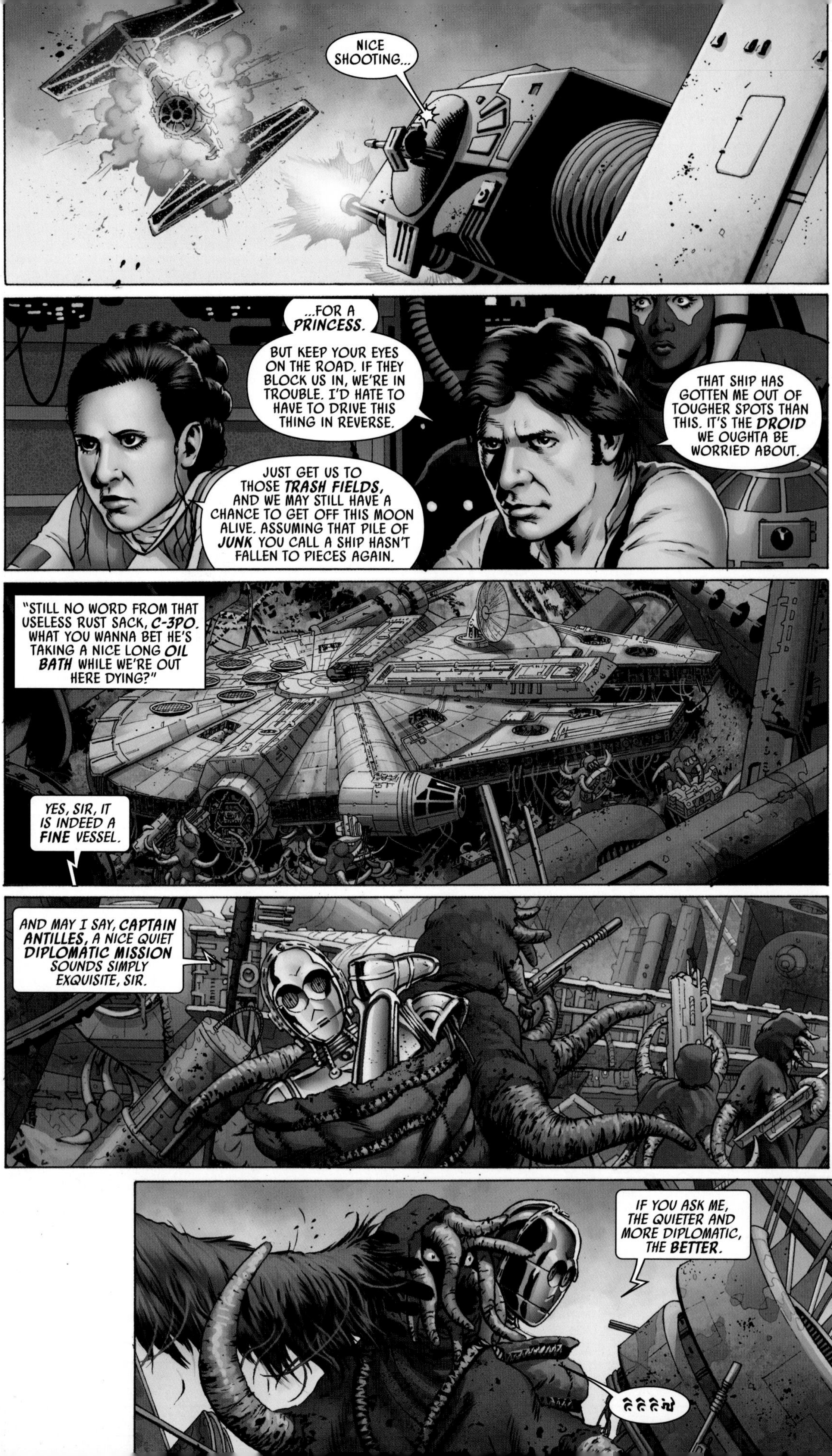

NICE SHOOTING...
...FOR A PRINCESS.
BUT KEEP YOUR EYES ON THE ROAD. IF THEY BLOCK US IN, WE'RE IN TROUBLE. I'D HATE TO HAVE TO DRIVE THIS THING IN REVERSE.
JUST GET US TO THOSE TRASH FIELDS, AND WE MAY STILL HAVE A CHANCE TO GET OFF THIS MOON ALIVE. ASSUMING THAT PILE OF JUNK YOU CALL A SHIP HASN'T FALLEN TO PIECES AGAIN.
THAT SHIP HAS GOTTEN ME OUT OF TOUGHER SPOTS THAN THIS. IT'S THE DROID WE OUGHTA BE WORRIED ABOUT.
"STILL NO WORD FROM THAT USELESS RUST SACK, C-3PO. WHAT YOU WANNA BET HE'S TAKING A NICE LONG OIL BATH WHILE WE'RE OUT HERE DYING?"
YES, SIR, IT IS INDEED A FINE VESSEL.
AND MAY I SAY, CAPTAIN ANTILLES, A NICE QUIET DIPLOMATIC MISSION SOUNDS SIMPLY EXQUISITE, SIR.
IF YOU ASK ME, THE QUIETER AND MORE DIPLOMATIC, THE BETTER.

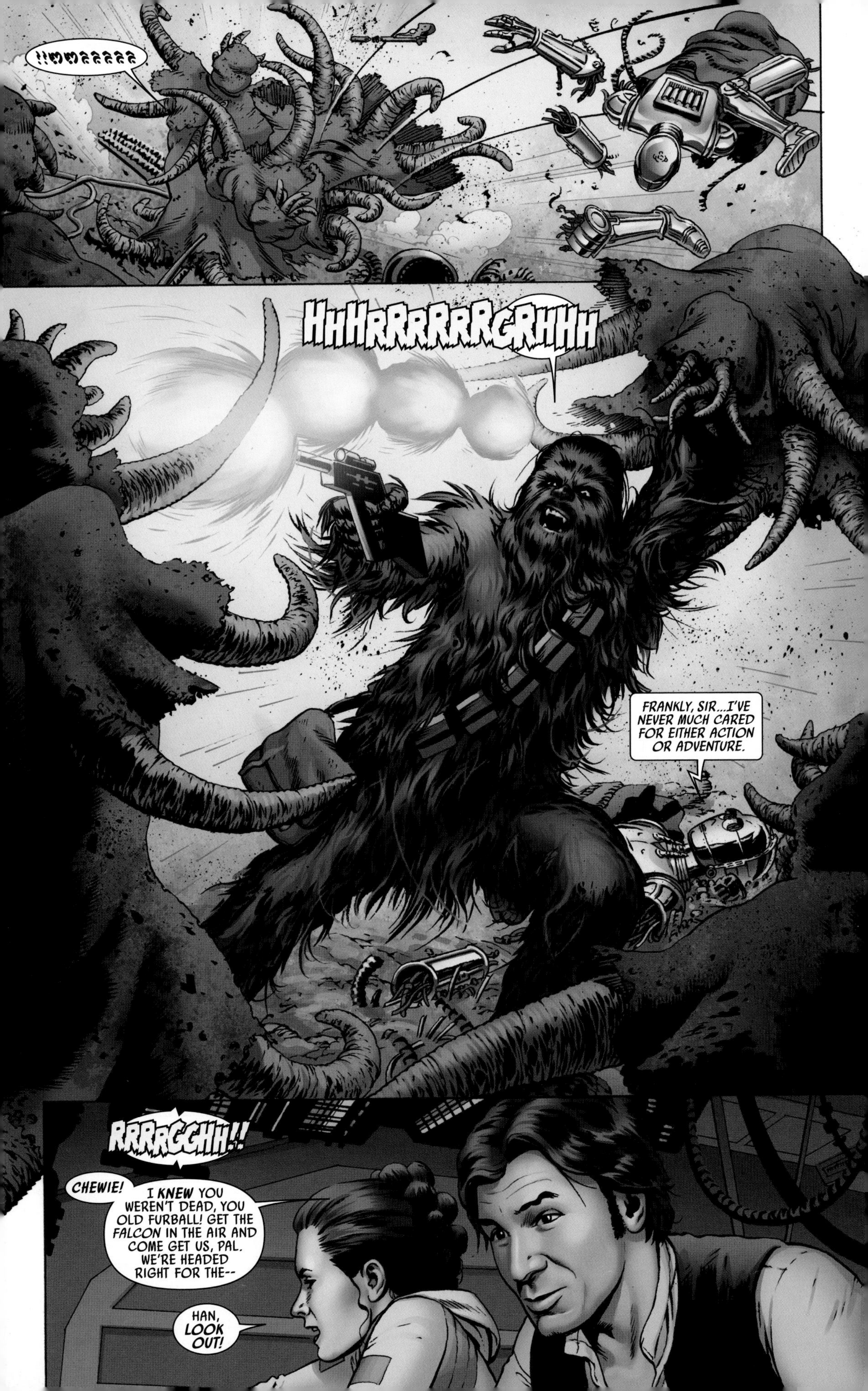
AAAAAAWW!!
HHHRRRRRRGRHHH
FRANKLY, SIR...I'VE NEVER MUCH CARED FOR EITHER ACTION OR ADVENTURE.
RRRRGGHH!!
CHEWIE!
I KNEW YOU WEREN'T DEAD, YOU OLD FURBALL! GET THE FALCON IN THE AIR AND COME GET US, PAL. WE'RE HEADED RIGHT FOR THE--
HAN, LOOK OUT!

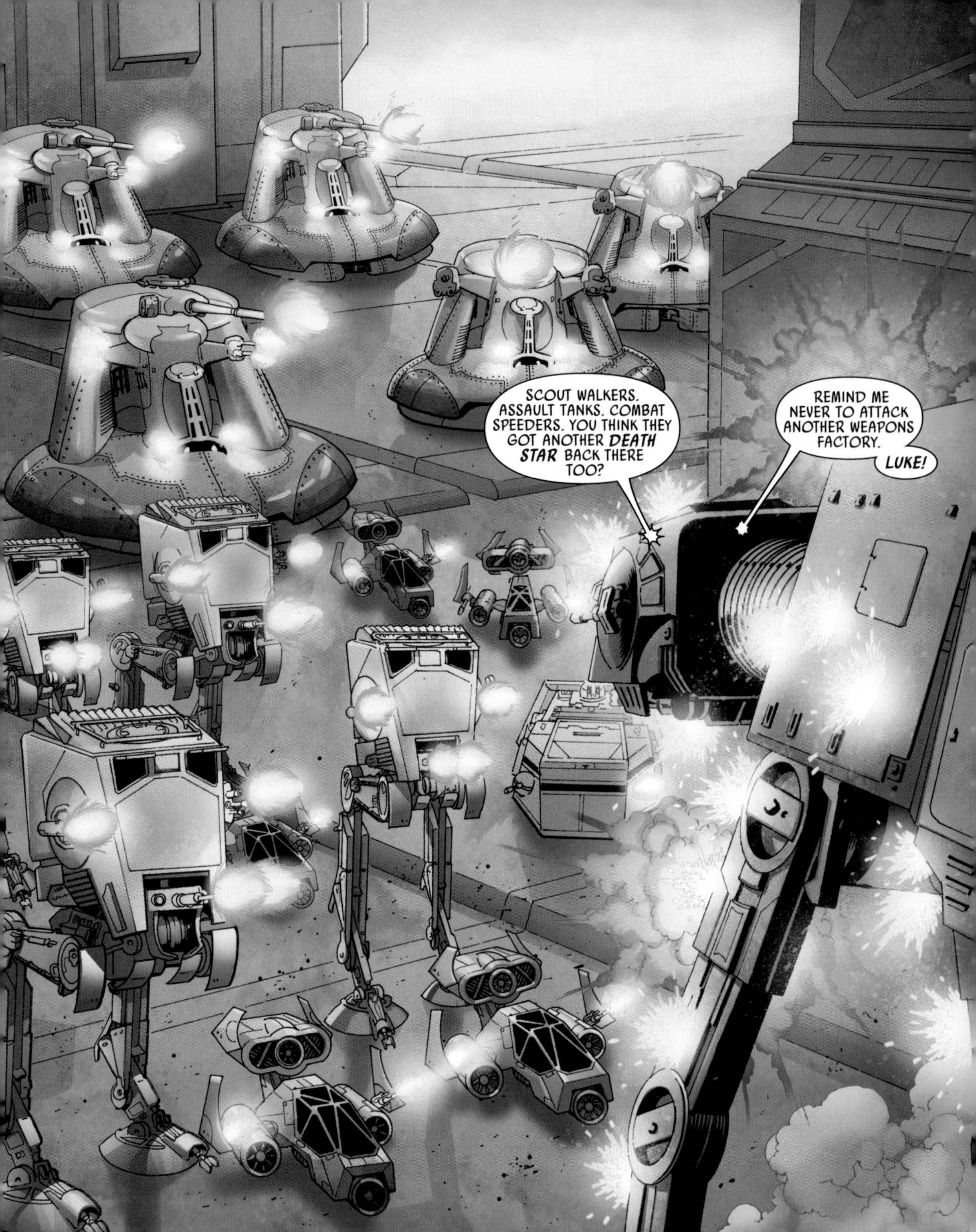
SCOUT WALKERS. ASSAULT TANKS. COMBAT SPEEDERS. YOU THINK THEY GOT ANOTHER DEATH STAR BACK THERE TOO?
REMIND ME NEVER TO ATTACK ANOTHER WEAPONS FACTORY.
LUKE!

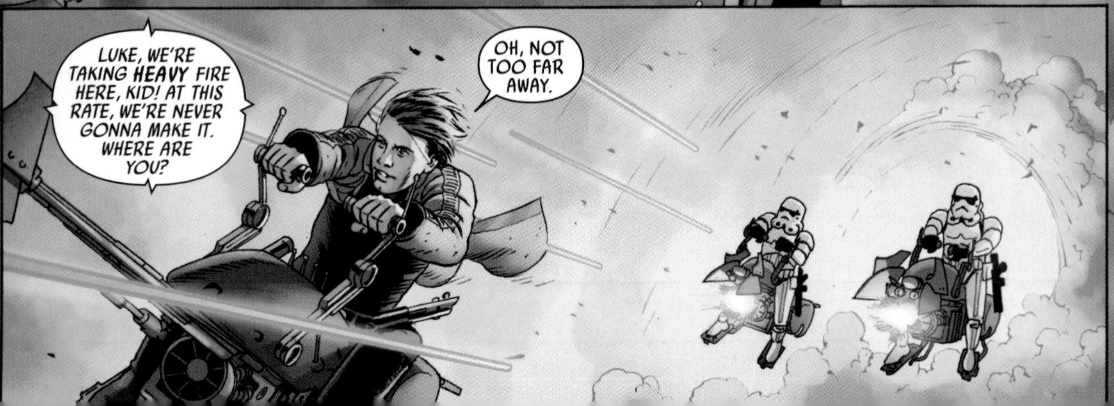
LUKE, WE'RE TAKING HEAVY FIRE HERE, KID! AT THIS RATE, WE'RE NEVER GONNA MAKE IT. WHERE ARE YOU?
OH, NOT TOO FAR AWAY.

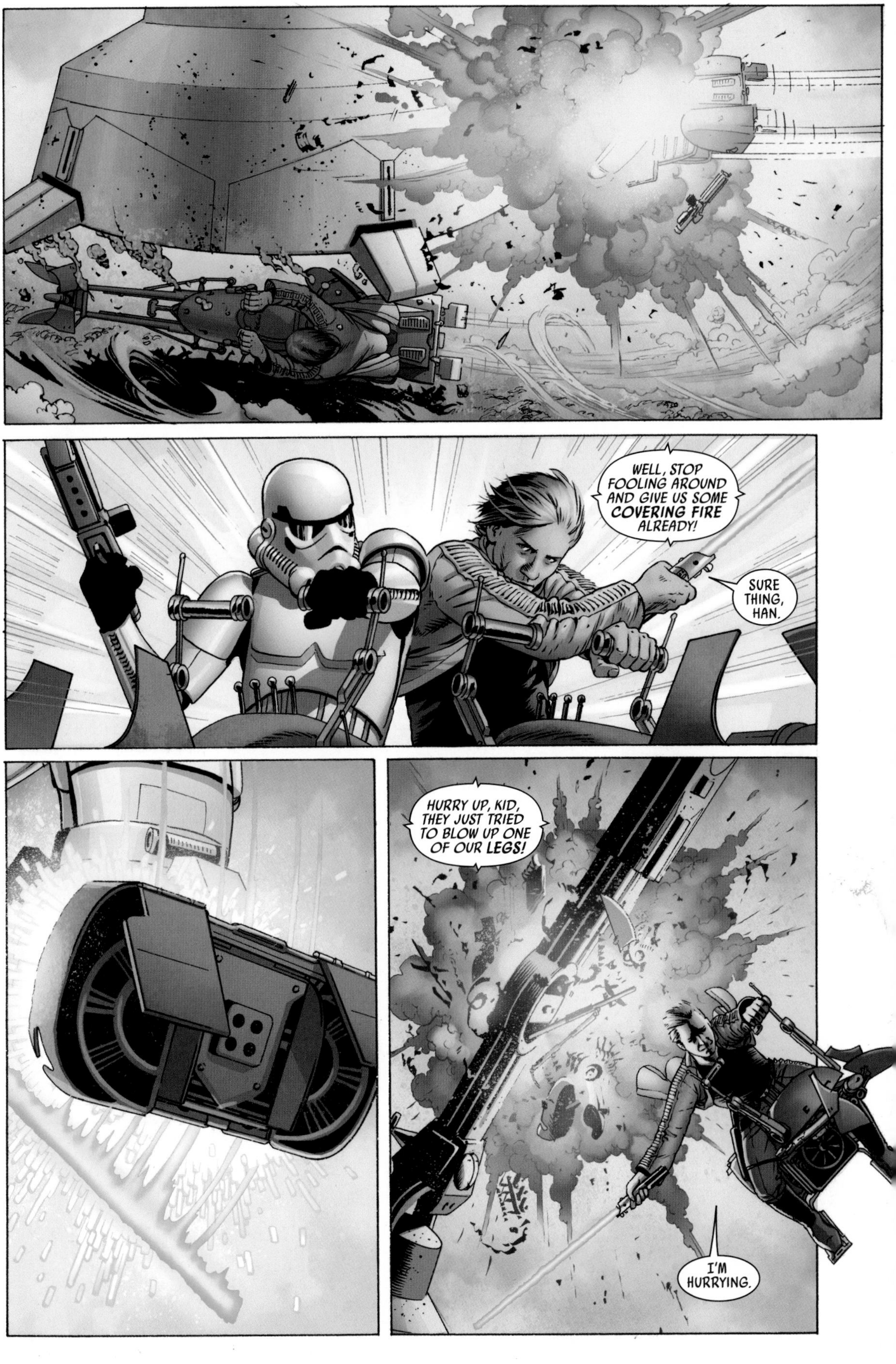
WELL, STOP FOOLING AROUND AND GIVE US SOME COVERING FIRE ALREADY!
SURE THING, HAN.
HURRY UP, KID, THEY JUST TRIED TO BLOW UP ONE OF OUR LEGS!
I'M HURRYING.

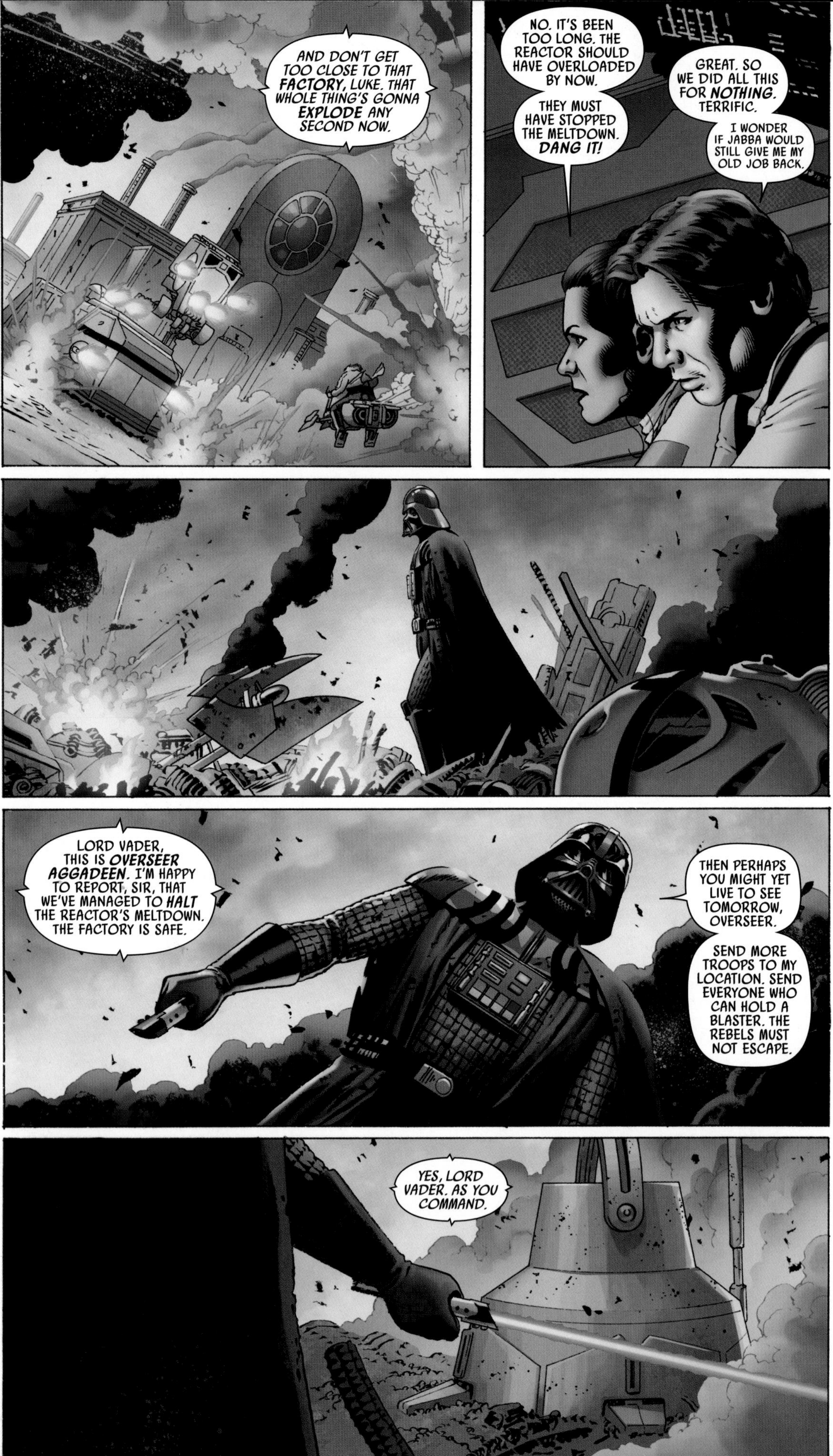
AND DON'T GET TOO CLOSE TO THAT FACTORY, LUKE. THAT WHOLE THING'S GONNA EXPLODE ANY SECOND NOW.
NO. IT'S BEEN TOO LONG. THE REACTOR SHOULD HAVE OVERLOADED BY NOW.
THEY MUST HAVE STOPPED THE MELTDOWN. DANG IT!
GREAT. SO WE DID ALL THIS FOR NOTHING. TERRIFIC.
I WONDER IF JABBA WOULD STILL GIVE ME MY OLD JOB BACK.
LORD VADER, THIS IS OVERSEER AGGADEEN. I'M HAPPY TO REPORT, SIR, THAT WE'VE MANAGED TO HALT THE REACTOR'S MELTDOWN. THE FACTORY IS SAFE.
THEN PERHAPS YOU MIGHT YET LIVE TO SEE TOMORROW, OVERSEER.
SEND MORE TROOPS TO MY LOCATION. SEND EVERYONE WHO CAN HOLD A BLASTER. THE REBELS MUST NOT ESCAPE.
YES, LORD VADER. AS YOU COMMAND.

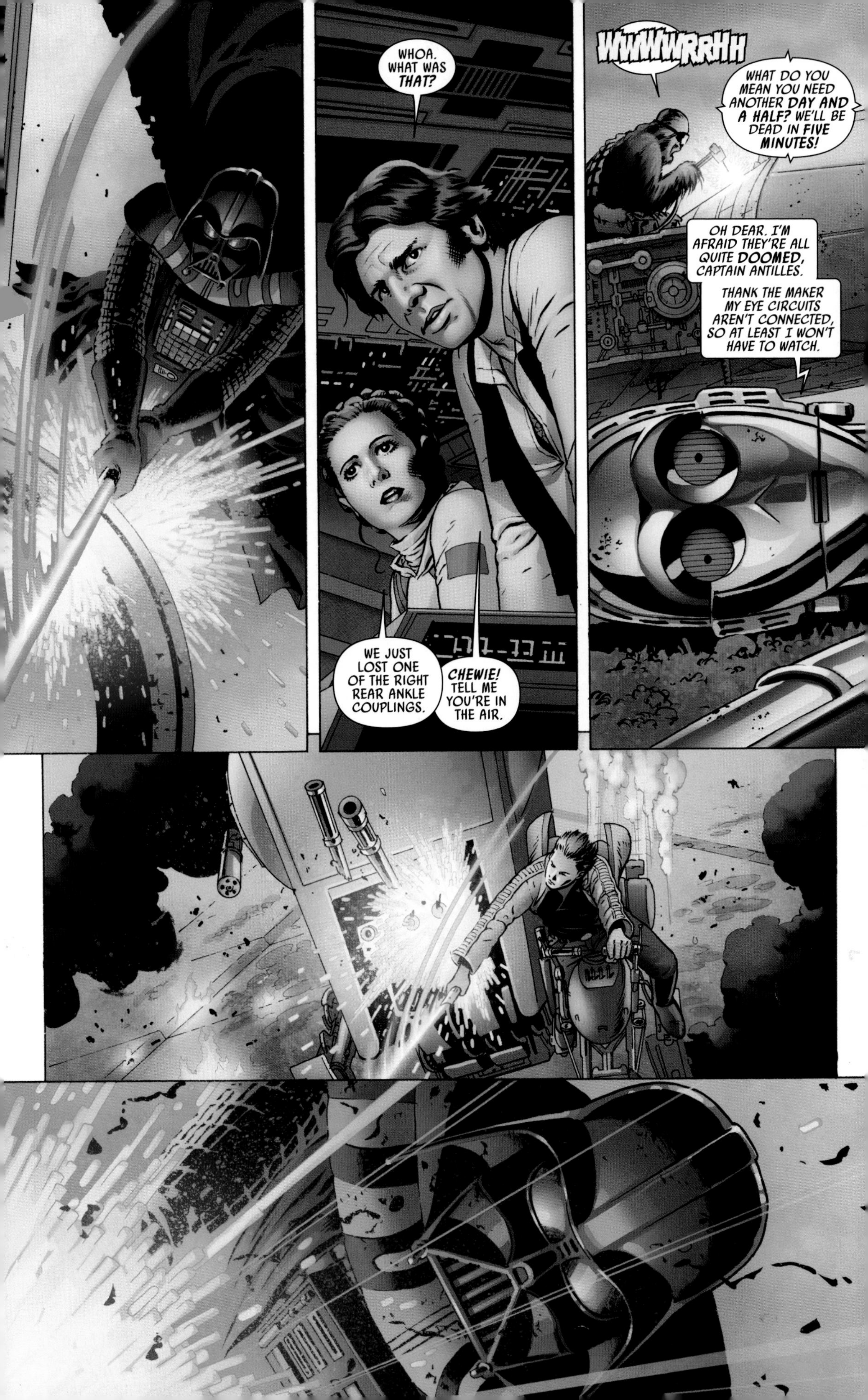
WHOA. WHAT WAS THAT?
WE JUST LOST ONE OF THE RIGHT REAR ANKLE COUPLINGS.
CHEWIE! TELL ME YOU'RE IN THE AIR.
WWWWRRHH
WHAT DO YOU MEAN YOU NEED ANOTHER DAY AND A HALF? WE'LL BE DEAD IN FIVE MINUTES!
OH DEAR. I'M AFRAID THEY'RE ALL QUITE DOOMED, CAPTAIN ANTILLES.
THANK THE MAKER MY EYE CIRCUITS AREN'T CONNECTED, SO AT LEAST I WON'T HAVE TO WATCH.

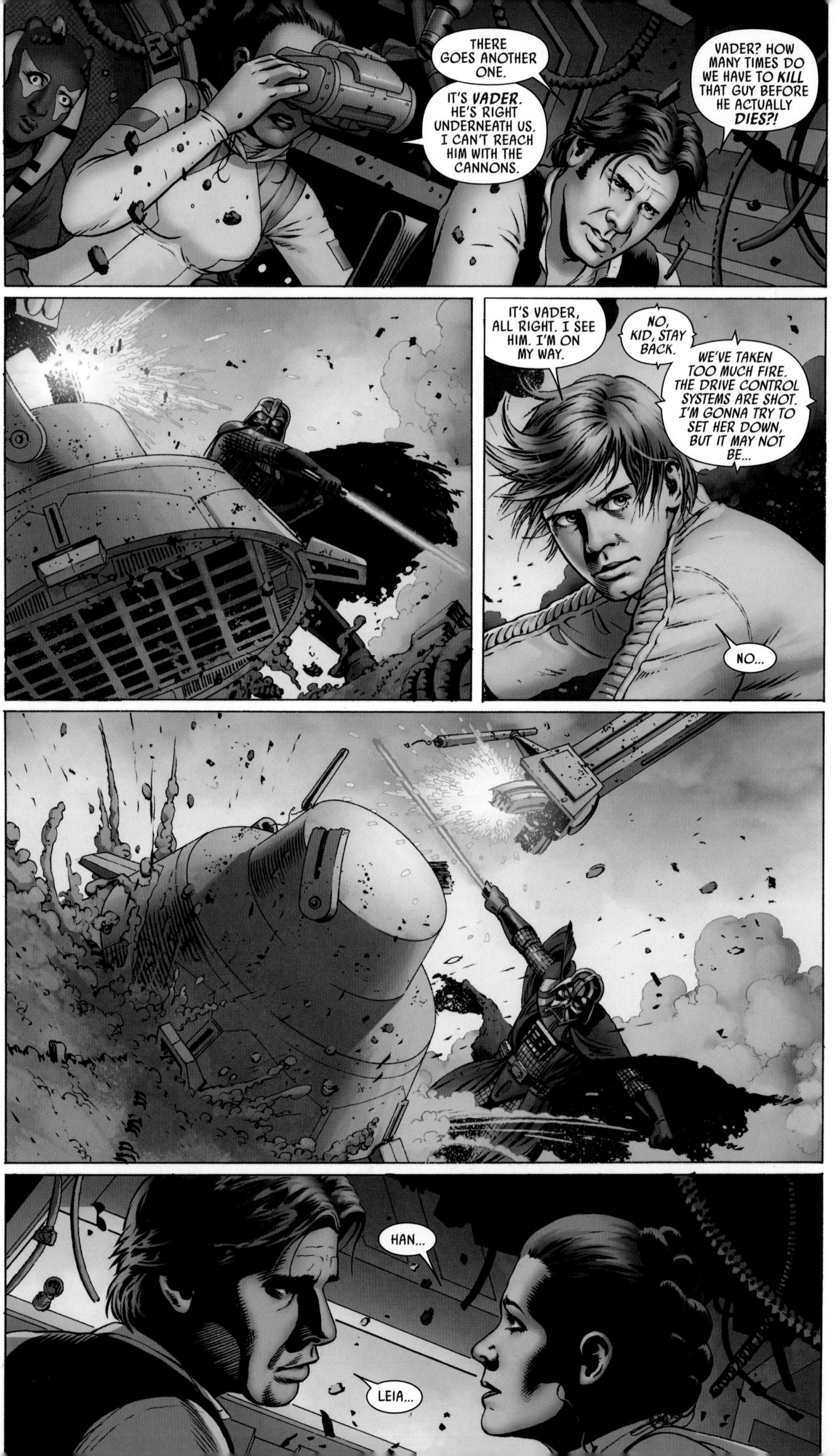
THERE GOES ANOTHER ONE.
IT'S **VADER**. HE'S RIGHT UNDERNEATH US. I CAN'T REACH HIM WITH THE CANNONS.
VADER? HOW MANY TIMES DO WE HAVE TO **KILL** THAT GUY BEFORE HE ACTUALLY **DIES?!**
IT'S VADER, ALL RIGHT. I SEE HIM. I'M ON MY WAY.
NO, KID, STAY BACK.
WE'VE TAKEN TOO MUCH FIRE. THE DRIVE CONTROL SYSTEMS ARE SHOT. I'M GONNA TRY TO SET HER DOWN, BUT IT MAY NOT BE...
NO...
HAN...
LEIA...

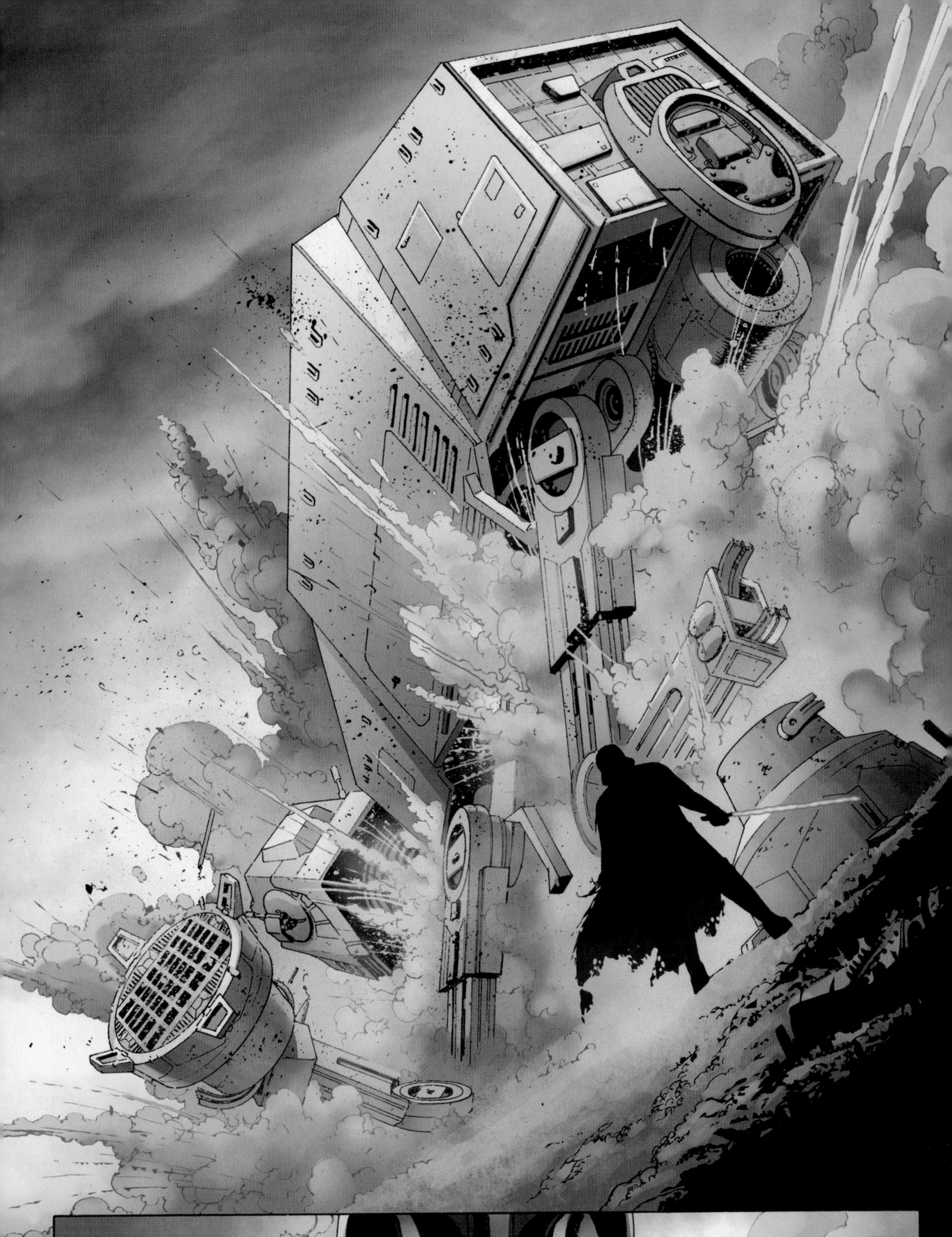

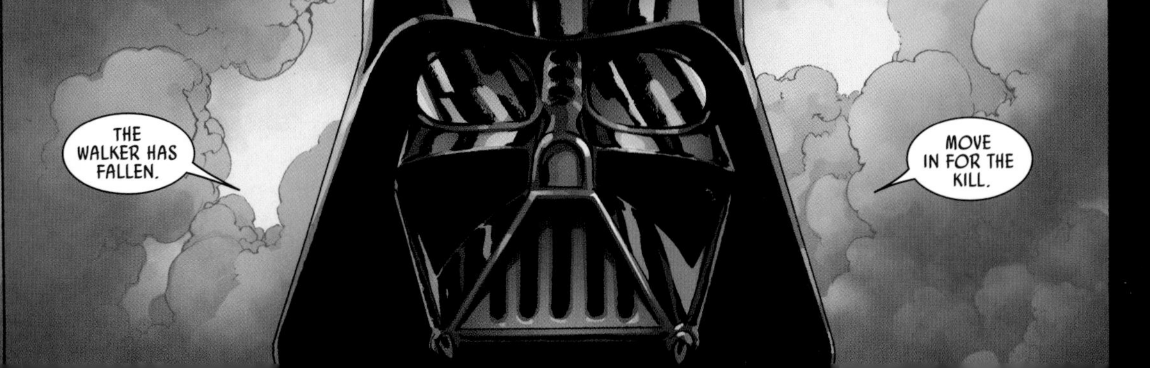
THE WALKER HAS FALLEN.
MOVE IN FOR THE KILL.

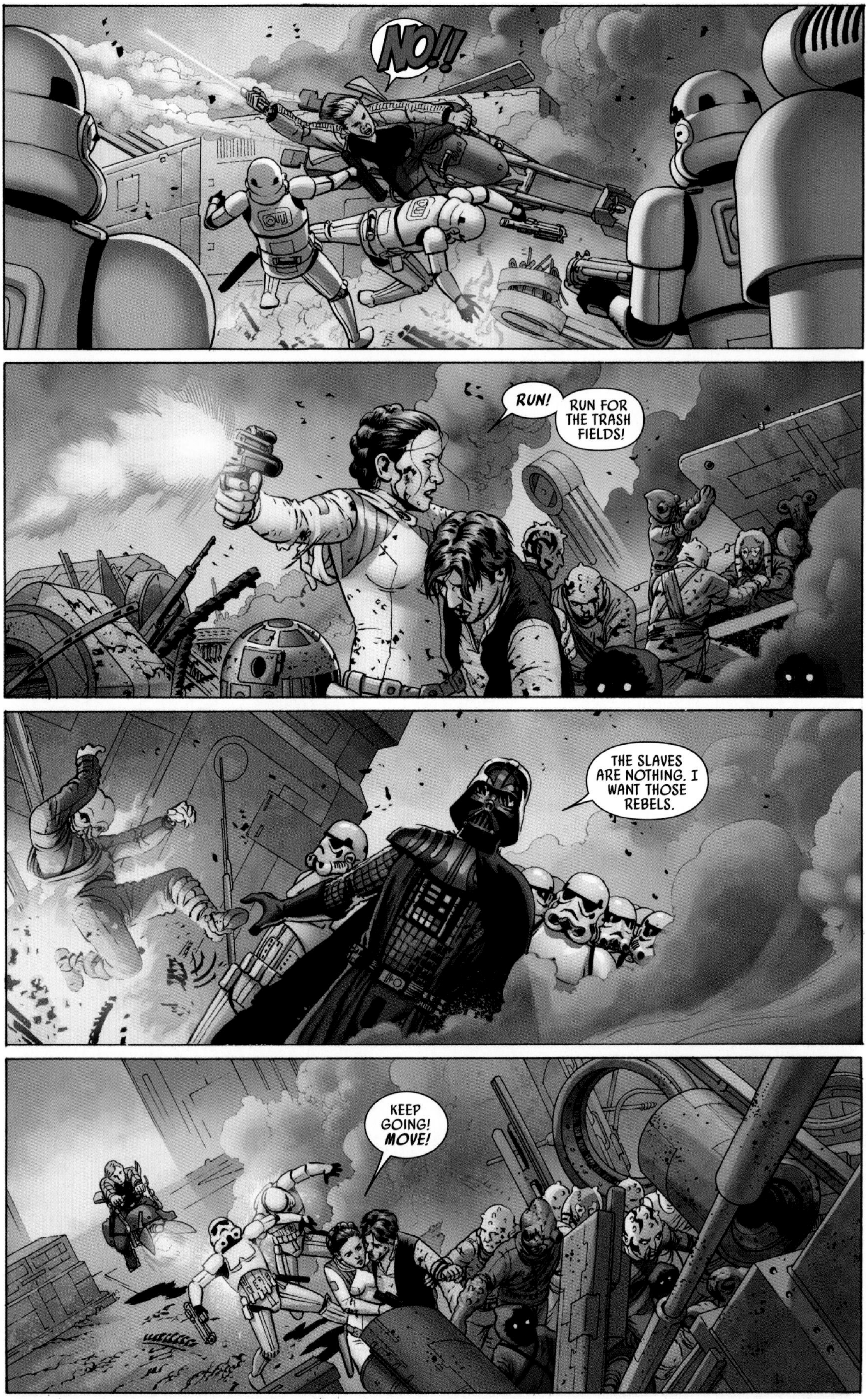
NO!!
RUN!
RUN FOR THE TRASH FIELDS!
THE SLAVES ARE NOTHING. I WANT THOSE REBELS.
KEEP GOING! MOVE!

LUKE! COME ON!

I CAN'T, LEIA. I CAN'T LET THIS ALL BE FOR NOTHING.

LUKE, GET OFF THAT SPEEDER! THAT'S AN ORDER!

DON'T WAIT FOR ME.

LUKE!

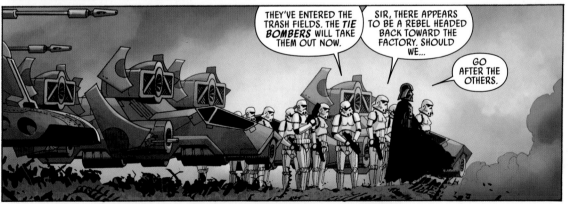

THEY'VE ENTERED THE TRASH FIELDS. THE *TIE BOMBERS* WILL TAKE THEM OUT NOW.

SIR, THERE APPEARS TO BE A REBEL HEADED BACK TOWARD THE FACTORY. SHOULD WE...

GO AFTER THE OTHERS.

HUGGH

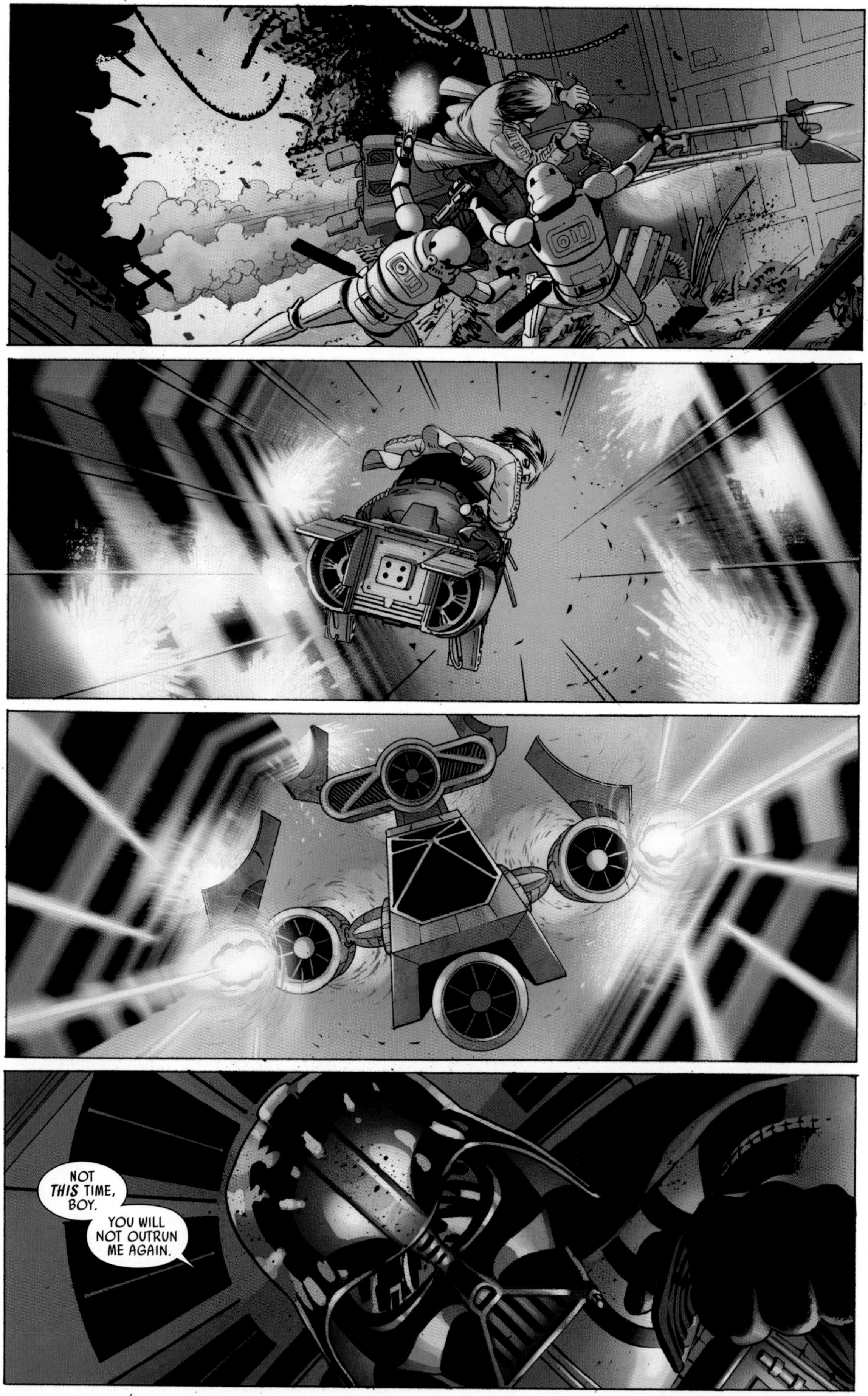
NOT THIS TIME, BOY.
YOU WILL NOT OUTRUN ME AGAIN.

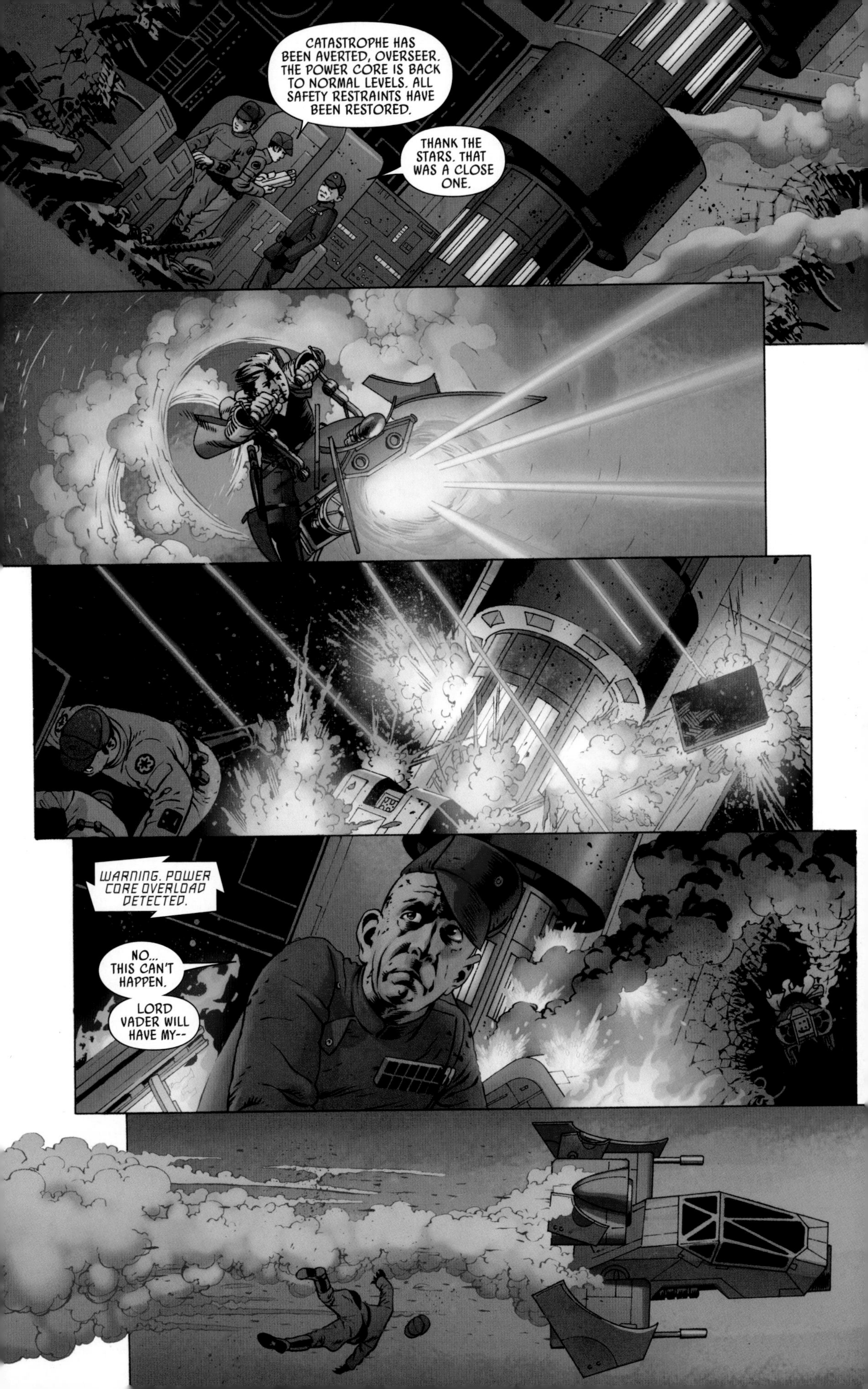
CATASTROPHE HAS BEEN AVERTED, OVERSEER. THE POWER CORE IS BACK TO NORMAL LEVELS. ALL SAFETY RESTRAINTS HAVE BEEN RESTORED.
THANK THE STARS. THAT WAS A CLOSE ONE.
WARNING. POWER CORE OVERLOAD DETECTED.
NO... THIS CAN'T HAPPEN.
LORD VADER WILL HAVE MY--

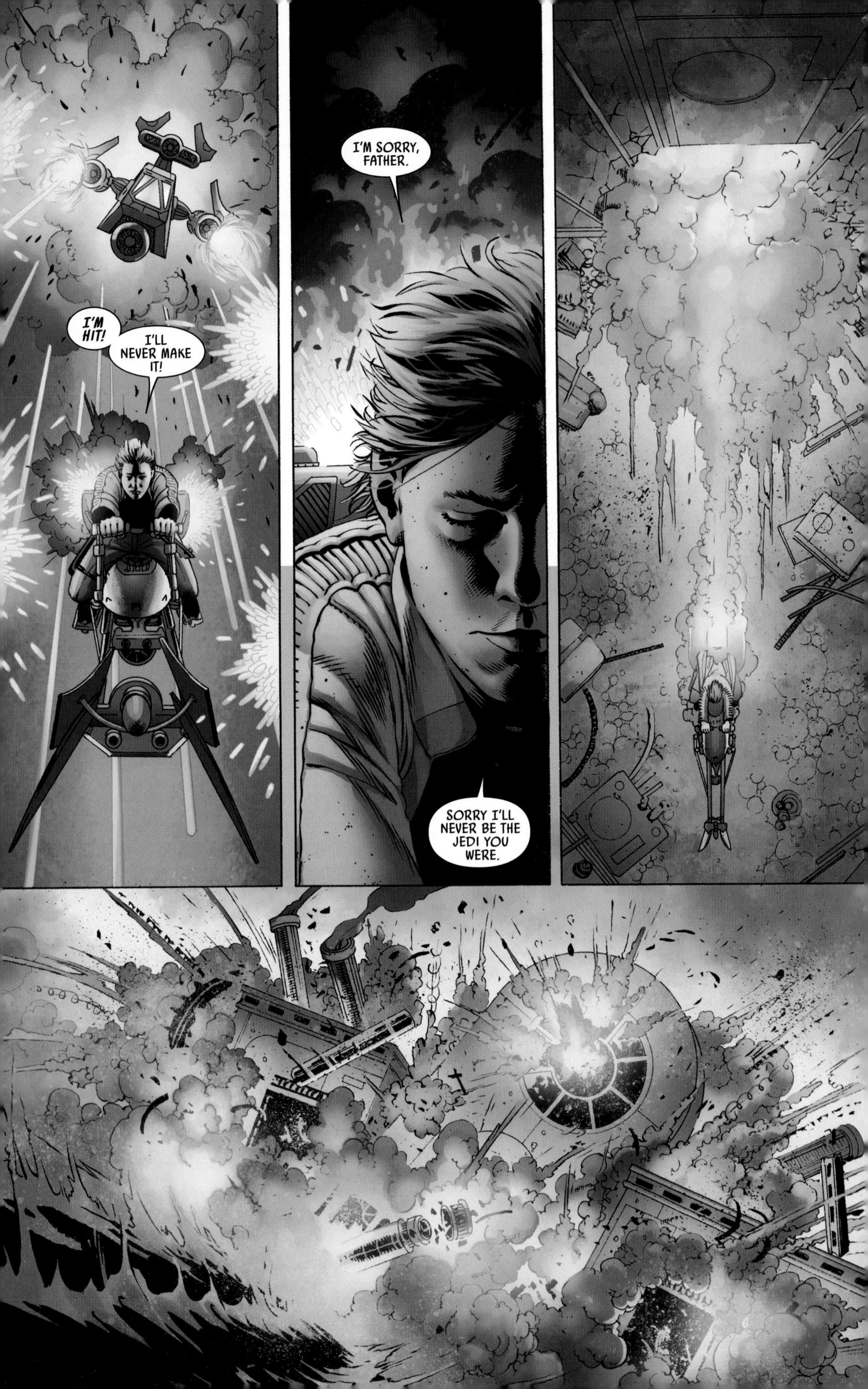

I'M HIT!
I'LL NEVER MAKE IT!
I'M SORRY, FATHER.
SORRY I'LL NEVER BE THE JEDI YOU WERE.

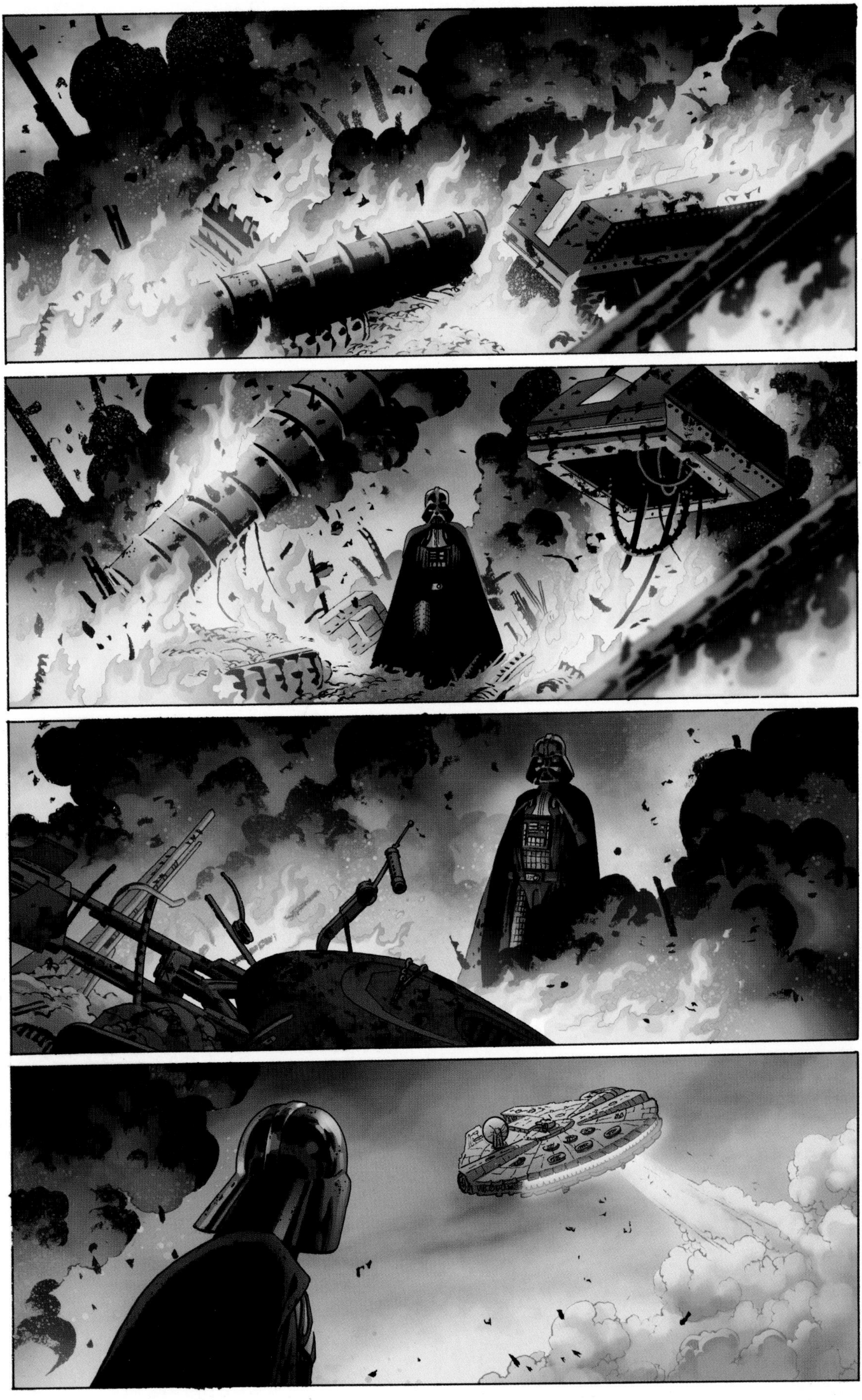

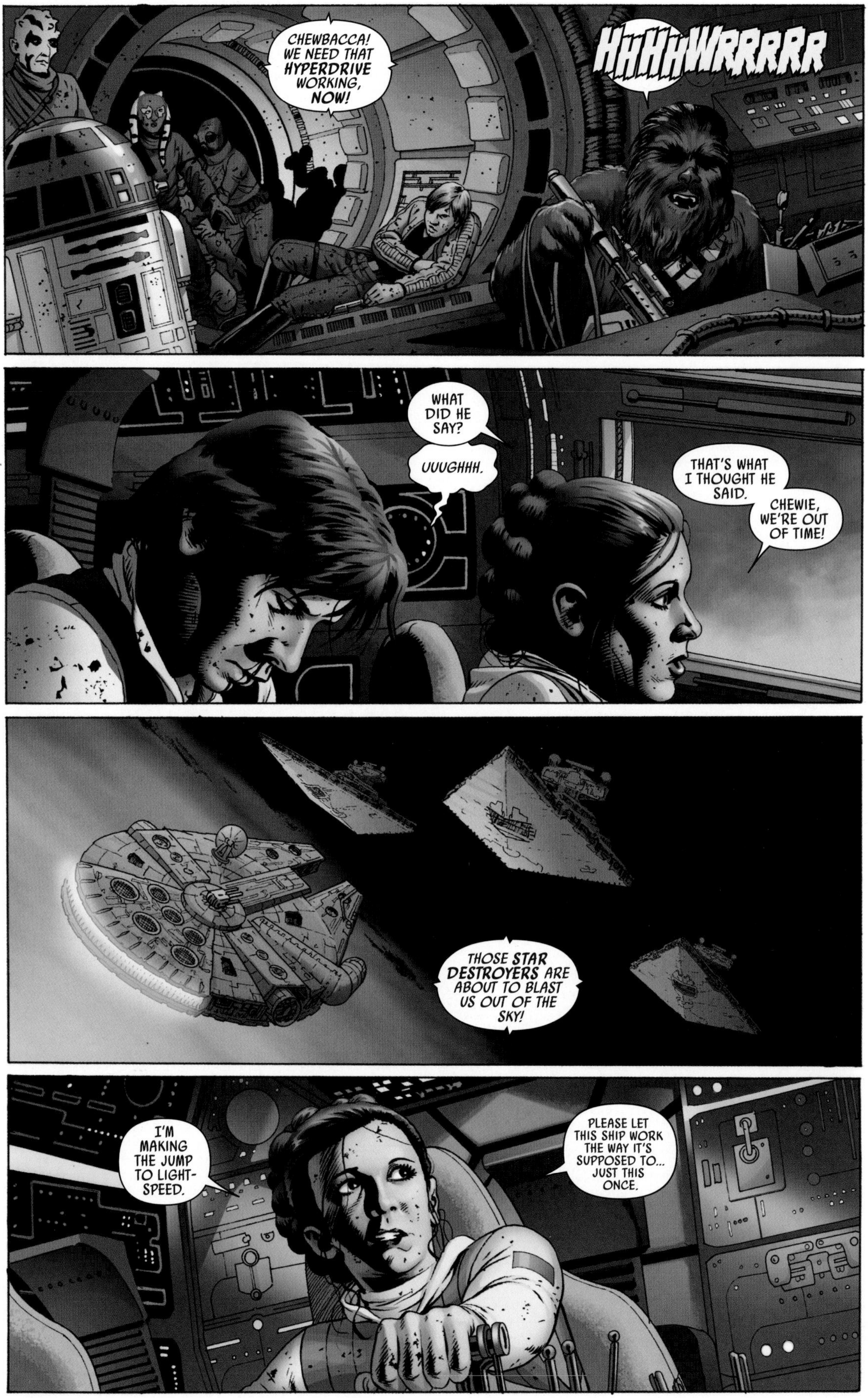
CHEWBACCA! WE NEED THAT HYPERDRIVE WORKING, NOW!
HHHHWRRRRR
WHAT DID HE SAY?
UUUGHHH.
THAT'S WHAT I THOUGHT HE SAID.
CHEWIE, WE'RE OUT OF TIME!
THOSE STAR DESTROYERS ARE ABOUT TO BLAST US OUT OF THE SKY!
I'M MAKING THE JUMP TO LIGHT-SPEED.
PLEASE LET THIS SHIP WORK THE WAY IT'S SUPPOSED TO... JUST THIS ONCE.

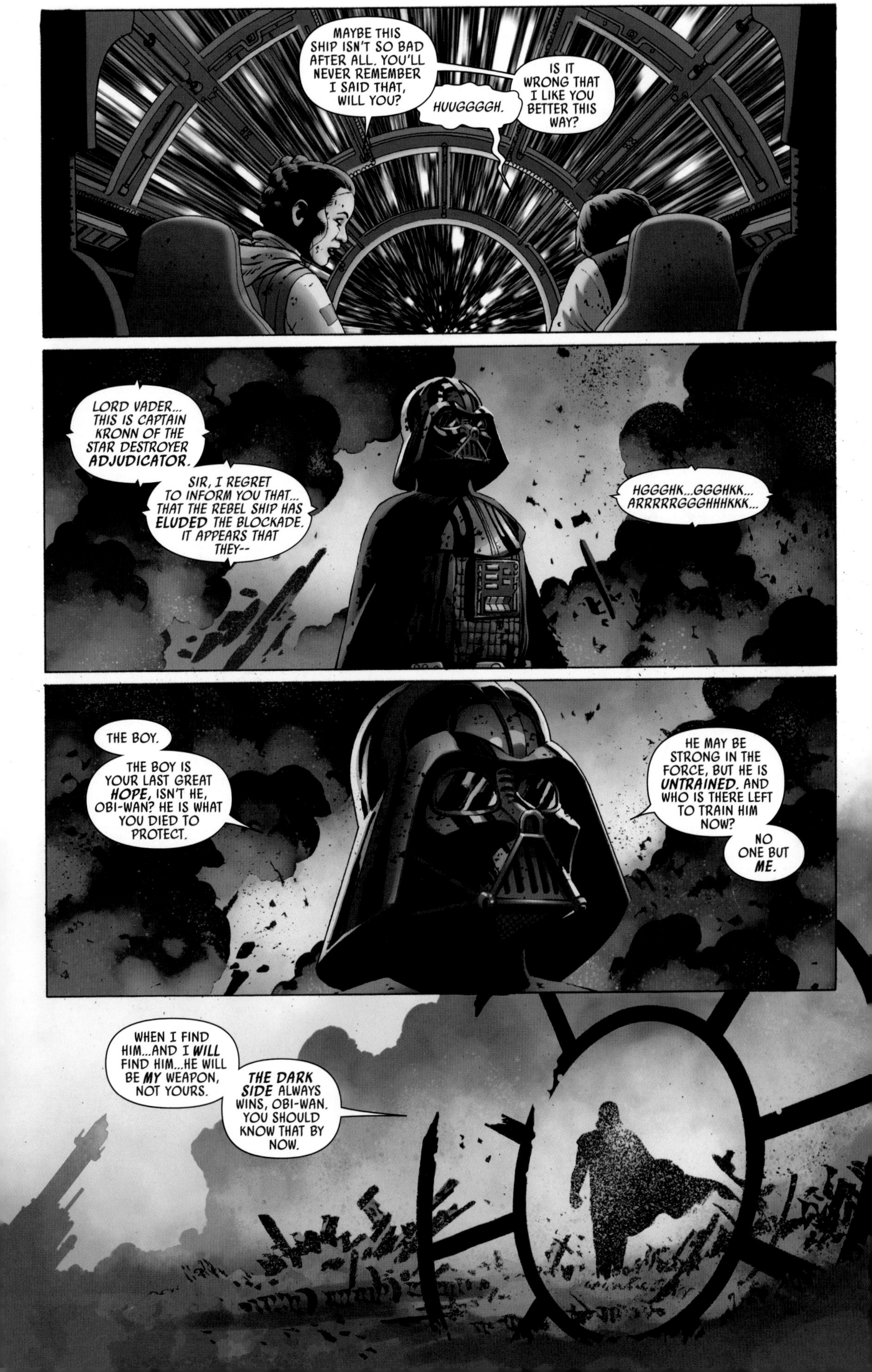
MAYBE THIS SHIP ISN'T SO BAD AFTER ALL. YOU'LL NEVER REMEMBER I SAID THAT, WILL YOU?
IS IT WRONG THAT I LIKE YOU BETTER THIS WAY?
HUUGGGGH.
LORD VADER... THIS IS CAPTAIN KRONN OF THE STAR DESTROYER ADJUDICATOR.
SIR, I REGRET TO INFORM YOU THAT... THAT THE REBEL SHIP HAS ELUDED THE BLOCKADE. IT APPEARS THAT THEY--
HGGGHK...GGGHKK... ARRRRRGGGHHHKKK...
THE BOY.
THE BOY IS YOUR LAST GREAT HOPE, ISN'T HE, OBI-WAN? HE IS WHAT YOU DIED TO PROTECT.
HE MAY BE STRONG IN THE FORCE, BUT HE IS UNTRAINED. AND WHO IS THERE LEFT TO TRAIN HIM NOW?
NO ONE BUT ME.
WHEN I FIND HIM...AND I WILL FIND HIM...HE WILL BE MY WEAPON, NOT YOURS.
THE DARK SIDE ALWAYS WINS, OBI-WAN. YOU SHOULD KNOW THAT BY NOW.

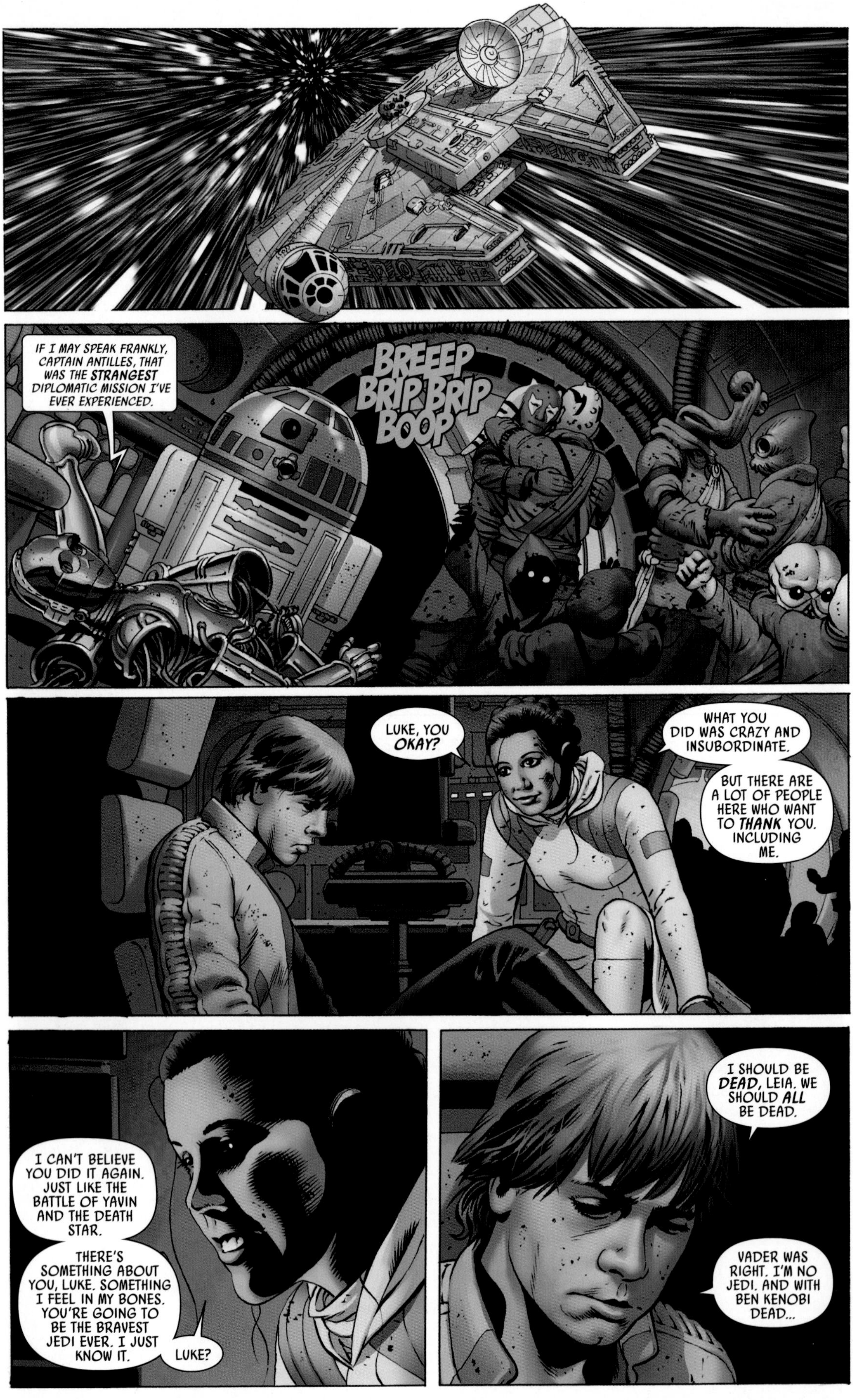
IF I MAY SPEAK FRANKLY, CAPTAIN ANTILLES, THAT WAS THE **STRANGEST** DIPLOMATIC MISSION I'VE EVER EXPERIENCED.
BREEEP BRIP BRIP BOOP
LUKE, YOU **OKAY?**
WHAT YOU DID WAS CRAZY AND INSUBORDINATE.
BUT THERE ARE A LOT OF PEOPLE HERE WHO WANT TO **THANK** YOU. INCLUDING ME.
I CAN'T BELIEVE YOU DID IT AGAIN. JUST LIKE THE BATTLE OF YAVIN AND THE DEATH STAR.
THERE'S SOMETHING ABOUT YOU, LUKE. SOMETHING I FEEL IN MY BONES. YOU'RE GOING TO BE THE BRAVEST JEDI EVER. I JUST KNOW IT.
LUKE?
I SHOULD BE **DEAD,** LEIA. WE SHOULD **ALL** BE DEAD.
VADER WAS RIGHT. I'M NO JEDI. AND WITH BEN KENOBI DEAD...

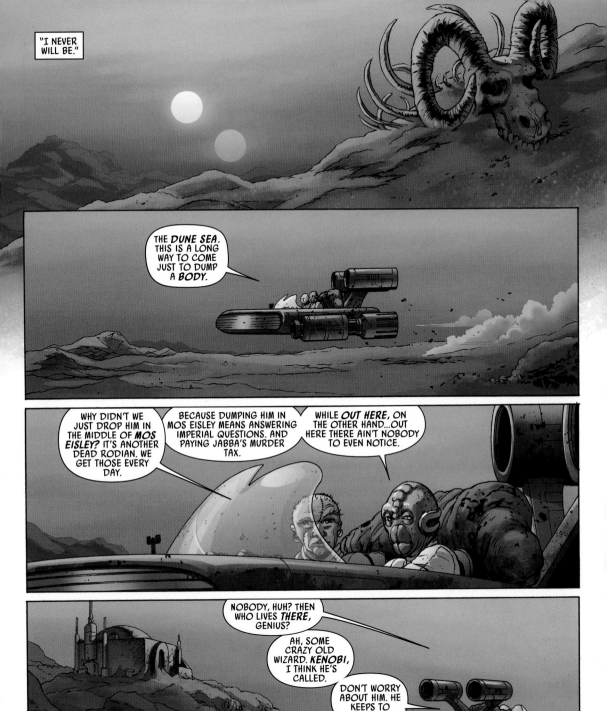

"I NEVER WILL BE."

THE *DUNE SEA.* THIS IS A LONG WAY TO COME JUST TO DUMP A *BODY.*

WHY DIDN'T WE JUST DROP HIM IN THE MIDDLE OF *MOS EISLEY?* IT'S ANOTHER DEAD RODIAN. WE GET THOSE EVERY DAY.

BECAUSE DUMPING HIM IN MOS EISLEY MEANS ANSWERING IMPERIAL QUESTIONS. AND PAYING JABBA'S MURDER TAX.

WHILE *OUT HERE,* ON THE OTHER HAND...OUT HERE THERE AIN'T NOBODY TO EVEN NOTICE.

NOBODY, HUH? THEN WHO LIVES *THERE,* GENIUS?

AH, SOME CRAZY OLD WIZARD. *KENOBI,* I THINK HE'S CALLED.

DON'T WORRY ABOUT HIM. HE KEEPS TO HIMSELF.

JUST KEEP AN EYE OUT FOR *SAND PEOPLE.*

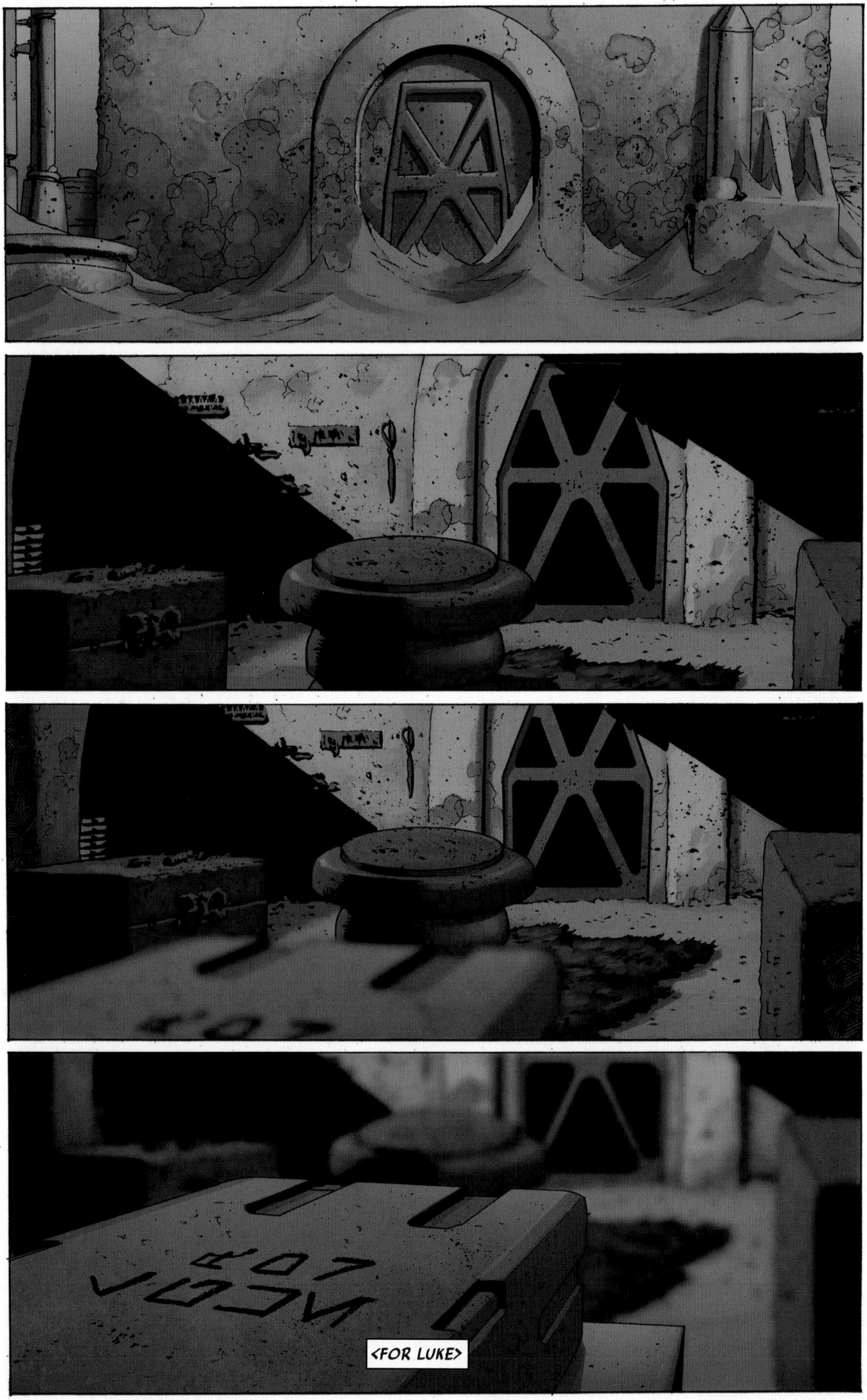
<FOR LUKE>

STAR WARS®

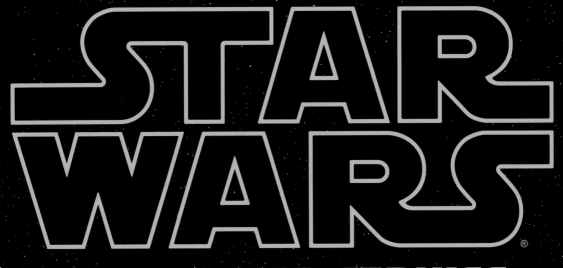

SKYWALKER STRIKES

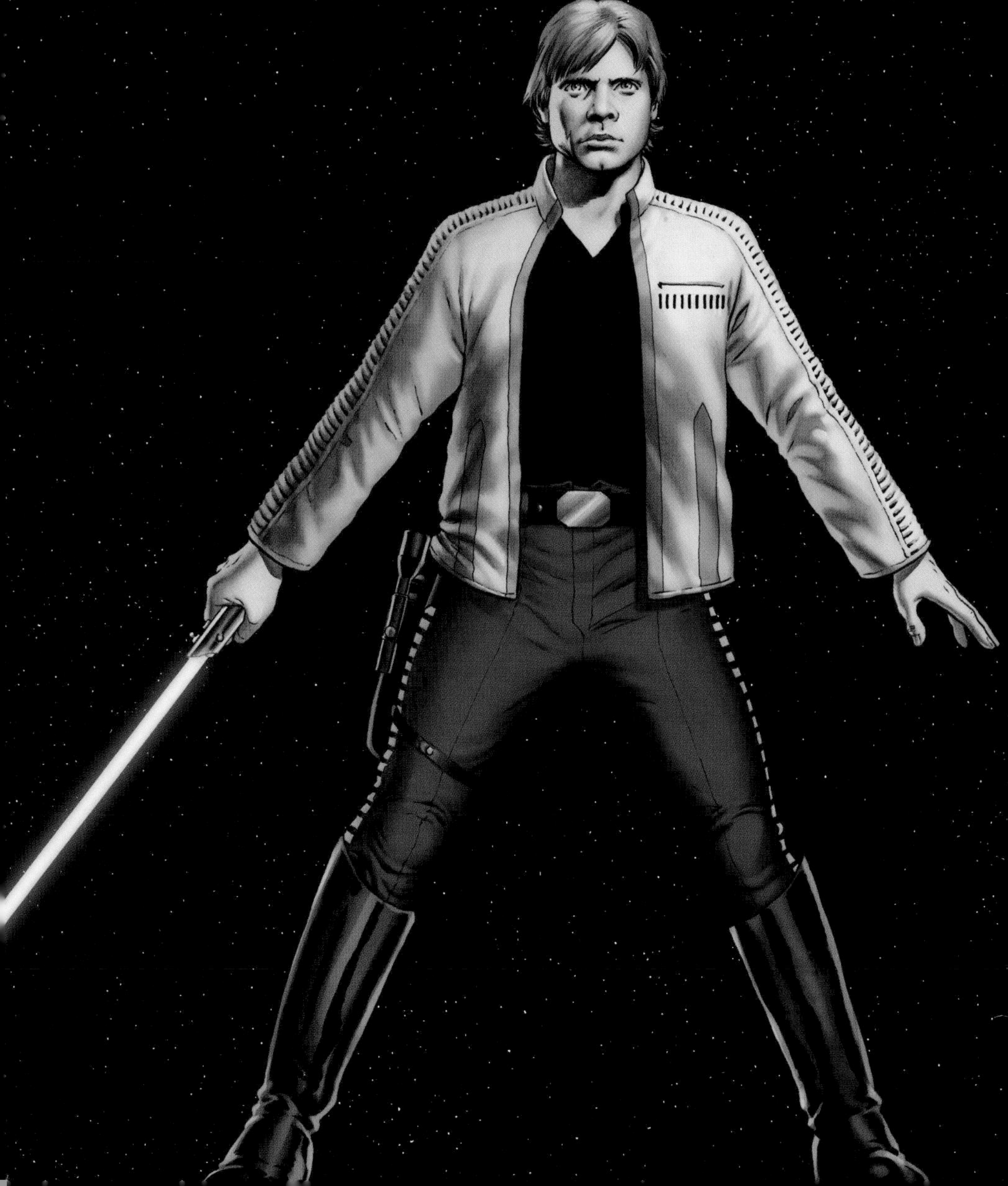

STAR WARS

SKYWALKER STRIKES

COLLECT THEM ALL!

Set of 6 Hardcover Books ISBN: 978-1-61479-526-1

STAR WARS
STAR WARS
SKYWALKER STRIKES: VOLUME 1
AARON CASSADAY MARTIN

Hardcover Book ISBN
978-1-61479-527-8

STAR WARS
STAR WARS
SKYWALKER STRIKES: VOLUME 2
AARON CASSADAY MARTIN

Hardcover Book ISBN
978-1-61479-528-5

STAR WARS
STAR WARS
SKYWALKER STRIKES: VOLUME 3
AARON CASSADAY MARTIN

Hardcover Book ISBN
978-1-61479-529-2

STAR WARS
STAR WARS
SKYWALKER STRIKES: VOLUME 4
AARON CASSADAY MARTIN

Hardcover Book ISBN
978-1-61479-530-8

STAR WARS
STAR WARS
SKYWALKER STRIKES: VOLUME 5
AARON CASSADAY MARTIN

Hardcover Book ISBN
978-1-61479-531-5

STAR WARS
STAR WARS
SKYWALKER STRIKES: VOLUME 6
AARON CASSADAY MARTIN

Hardcover Book ISBN
978-1-61479-532-2

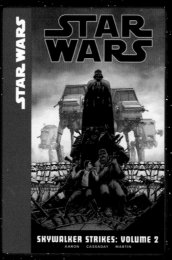

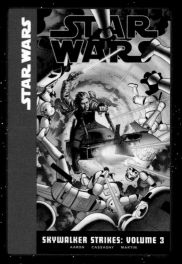

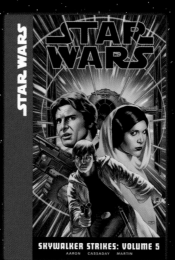

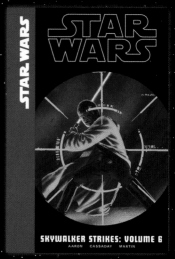